RUTHANN AND HER PIG

A Richard Jackson Book

RUTHANN AND HER PIG

Barbara Ann Porte

Pictures by

Suçie Stevenson

Orchard Books   New York

A division of Franklin Watts, Inc.

Orchard Books, A division of Franklin Watts, Inc.
387 Park Avenue South, New York, NY 10016

Orchard Books Canada
20 Torbay Road, Markham, Ontario 23P 1G6

Manufactured in the United States of America
Book design by Mina Greenstein
The text of this book is set in 12 pt. Aster
The illustrations are watercolor, reproduced in full color
10 9 8 7 6 5 4 3 2 1

Library of Congress Cataloging-in-Publication Data
Porte, Barbara Ann. Ruthann and her pig / Barbara Ann
Porte ; illustrated by Suçie Stevenson. p.   cm.
Summary: While visiting his cousin Ruthann in the coun-
try, Frank decides that her pet pig Henry Brown would be
the perfect companion to ride with him on the school bus
for protection against wild older kids.
ISBN 0-531-05825-5. ISBN 0-531-08425-6 (lib. bdg.)
[1. Pigs—Fiction. 2. Cousins—Fiction.] I. Stevenson,
Suçie, ill. II. Title.
PZ7.P7995Ru 1989 [Fic]—dc19 88-31452 CIP AC

This book is for
Ashley Christine Thomas
and, again, for
Alexandra.

Contents

1
Ruthann and Her Pig

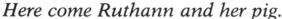

Here come Ruthann and her pig.

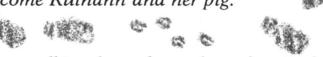

They are walking down the road together. Ruthann is in front. They pass by Ruthann's mother. She is working in her garden. She is on her hands and knees, pulling up the weeds around her roses.

"Hi, Mam," Ruthann says.

"Hi, Ruthann," her mam replies. "Hi, pig."

Ruthann's mam believes it is important for a mother to take an interest in her daughter's pet, even if it is a pig, even if she thinks a cat would be a better pet. Almost anything, she thinks, would be better than a pig. This minute, though, she only hopes that Ruthann's pig won't step on any of her roses.

"Its name is Ernestine," Ruthann tells her, referring to the pig.

"Right," says her mam, who always calls it "pig," regardless. Today its name is Ernestine, but Ruthann's mother knows that yesterday its name was Herman. She thought Herman was a fine name for a pig. Short and to the point. Also, she believes that Ruthann's pig is a boy. Herman is certainly a better name than Ernestine for a boy pig. Not that it matters. Tomorrow the pig will probably have a new name altogether.

"It's only a stage," Ruthann's mother and father tell each other. They hope she will outgrow it.

Ruthann waves goodbye to her mother and walks away with the pig.

"I have said it before, and I'll say it again," Ruthann's mother says to the roses. "A cat would be a better pet."

That night, after dinner, she brings the subject up.

"Petunia," she says, "would be a fine name for a cat."

"Whose cat?" asks Ruthann's father.

"Or for a kitten," she adds. "Kittens are so soft and so furry. They take up hardly any room. Much less room than a pig for instance. Also, kittens smell like kittens,

while a pig, however tidy, still always smells like a pig."
She prefers roses herself, but knows sometimes a
mother has to compromise.

Here come Ruthann and her pig and her cat.

They are walking single file beside the meadow. Ruthann can see her father haying in the field. Sometimes
Ruthann helps him. "Hey," her father says those times,
"we two are farmers in the field together."

"Hi, Dad," Ruthann says this time. The pig and the
cat are mum.

"Hi, Ruthie! Hi, Ernestine! Hi, Petunia!" says her
father. He makes a point of showing interest in his
daughter's pets. "How's that Ernestine doing today?"
he asks.

"His name is Franciswerner," Ruthann tells him.

Her father looks surprised. Perhaps he is surprised
to know a pig that has two names. Ruthann explains.
"Franciswerner," she explains, "is not a first and last
name. It is just one long name that's run together. The
same as Ruthann," she says.

Last year Ruthann's teacher couldn't understand it.
"Are you certain?" she had asked Ruthann. "Are you

positive it's all one name, and isn't spelled the normal way? Maybe," she suggested, hopefully, as though Ruthann just didn't have sense enough to know it, "Ruth is your first name and Ann is your middle one." The next day Ruthann brought a note from home.

"Ruthann's middle name," her mother wrote, "is Brodie." Ruthann would have liked to say, "Please, from now on call me Ruthann Brodie every day." She meant like Mary Ellen who was always called by both her first and middle names. But she kept her mouth closed so that it couldn't say that. Something told her, enough was enough.

"I see," Ruthann's father says now. He stares for a minute at the scarecrow in the field, then at the pig. "That's a nice pig you have," he tells Ruthann, "whatever its name. I take it you're all straight about the cat." He means about its name.

"Mam named her," says Ruthann, agreeing that it's final, though she doesn't see the point. Ruthann wishes she could sometimes change her own name. She especially wishes it when her father calls her Ruthie. She hates being called Ruthie, although she doesn't tell him that. She doesn't want to hurt his feelings. He's always so polite about her pig.

"Every person needs a nickname," says Ruthann's father now and then. His own name is Frederick, but his friends call him Fritz. Ruthann thinks if she could change her name this minute she would name herself Penelope—Penelope Packer. She would change her pig's name to Peter. That way her father could say: Penny Packer's pet pig Pete. Ruthann throws a kiss to her father, waves her hand, and walks away. The pig and the cat walk behind her.

"I have said it before and I'll say it again," her father says to the scarecrow. "A dog would be a better pet."

That night, after dinner, Ruthann's father brings the subject up. "I think what is missing on this farm is a pup. What do you think, Ruthann?" It is not the first time she's been asked this question. She looks up and then away, then over in the corner where her cat is curled beside the pig, both of them asleep. In other words, she doesn't answer. "Every child should have a dog," her father says just as if she had. "I had a dog when I was your age. Its name was Rover." It's an old story. Ruthann has heard it all before. Still she asks, "Rover, you called it Rover every day?" She is trying to hold up her end of the conversation. Her father nods.

"It's a good name for a dog," he says. Ruthann does not say what she thinks. She thinks, in the first place, that there are far too many dogs named Rover and, in the second place, that being called the same name every day is boring. To be called Rover for a lifetime is almost more than she can contemplate. Even so, she doesn't criticize, aware, as she is, that her father doesn't criticize her pig. Instead, she says, as she has said in the past, "I'm sure any dog would be proud to have such a name as Rover."

Her dad looks pleased to hear it.

Here come Ruthann and her pig and her cat and her dog.

Ruthann's grandmother is at the kitchen window watching. "Look, look," she says with excitement, as

much as she can muster at her age and disposition. She is nearly eighty and has been some places and has seen some things, believe me. "A parade is going by."

Ruthann's mother looks. Her hands are wet from washing dishes. She wipes them on her apron, which is not so much an apron as it is a smock with pockets for her clippers, pruners, trowels, dibbers, and other tools such as she uses in her garden. She raises more than roses; peanuts, beans, and squash are not beyond her. "That," she says, "is not a parade. It is only Ruthann going by with that pig and Petunia and her new dog named Rover."

Ruthann's grandmother puts on her eyeglasses. "I see," she says. "Ruthann," she calls through the window, "this is your grandmother. I've come for a visit." Ruthann's grandmother lives several farms away. She visits often and sleeps over.

"I see you're still trotting around with that pig," she says when Ruthann arrives in the kitchen. Ruthann's pig, and her cat, and her dog sit down together by the door. Ruthann's grandmother does not approve of animals in kitchens.

"If you ask me," she says to Ruthann's mother, who hasn't, "Ruthann needs a friend. An only child on a farm," she says. "I'm not surprised at whom she plays with." She means the pig. She can overlook the dog and cat, normal household pets, more or less. "What you want to do," she tells Ruthann's mother, "is to invite Frank's boy Frank to visit." She means Cousin Frank, Frank, Jr., her other son's son. "A boy like that would be good company for Ruthann. Also," she adds, "it would get him out of town. Town is no place to raise a boy." Ruthann's grandmother believes children should be raised in the country.

"THAT'S SOME PIG," Frank says the day that he arrives.

"Thank you," says Ruthann. "His name is Henry

Brown." A double name has a nice ring, she's decided, however it's spelled.

Here come Ruthann and her pig and her cat and her dog and her cousin Frank.

Her father calls him Sonny.

"Gezundheit, Sonny!" he says when they pass.

"Thank you," says Frank. "I think I'm coming down with a cold."

But he isn't. "He sounds the same to me as last time when he had his allergy attack," Ruthann's mother says that evening. Ruthann's father has given up saying "gezundheit." It's clear to him and everybody that Frank isn't in good health.

"Feathers make him wheeze," Frank's mother said that other time. "A good thing Ruthann has a pig and not a duck," their grandmother said. This time Ruthann's mother has put away all the feather pillows.

Over the telephone, and sounding worried, Frank's mother asks, "Is there something new at the farm?"

"Rover is new. Ruthann has a farm dog now," Ruthann's father says in a proud voice. "Well, she has a new cat, too," he adds. It's as though he's never heard of such a thing as an allergy. Ruthann's mother has. She puts her head in her hands and sighs. Why didn't she see it sooner? Feathers and fur, she thinks. Of course. A child allergic to one is often allergic to the other.

"Dog and cat? Dog and cat? You say you've got a dog and cat?" When Frank's mother, Ruthann's aunt Lydia, is upset her voice rises. Also, she repeats herself. "What happened to that nice pig Ruthann used to run around with?" she asks in her highest voice.

"It's a little bit complicated," Ruthann's mother says, having taken control of the telephone. "You mustn't upset yourself. I'm putting the dog and cat outside this minute. I think Frank is breathing better already. Don't you worry now."

"A fine thing," their grandmother says, turning in early for the night, "when it's the pig that gets to stay indoors."

Here come Ruthann and her pig and her cousin Frank.

The cat, Petunia, is cozy in the barn. Rover has attached himself to Ruthann's dad.

"Here Rover," her father called this morning. "I

10

could use this dog in the field," he said. Ruthann could not imagine for what. "A scarecrow is fine in its place," said her father, "but for company's sake, you can't beat a good dog like Rover." Rover looked up at Ruthann's father, wagged his tail, and grinned. If Ruthann had not seen it with her own two eyes, she would have said it was impossible.

"I think Henry Brown likes me," Frank says now to Ruthann. Ruthann nods, agreeing that it's so. "Can he

come home with me?" Frank asks. Of course he doesn't mean forever, but only for a visit. Perhaps a week or two.

Ruthann swallows hard. She is too astonished by his question to answer right away. "A pig," she points out in a while, "takes up a bit of space."

"We have a backyard and a lawn," says Frank. "Also a finished basement."

"A finished basement," Ruthann echoes, stalling for time, picturing how Henry Brown would look there. "Henry Brown," she tells Frank, "is a pure pet. I raised him from a piglet. I can't just send him off with you because you happen not to be allergic. Besides, he's getting older." She means that the older one gets, the less one likes change.

"Maybe he could come for Christmas," suggests Frank. "We could see how he likes it. If he likes it a lot, he could come back for spring recess. Both of you could. We have a guest room in the finished basement."

"We'll see," says Ruthann, the same way that her parents say it, meaning exactly what they mean by it.

"Gee, that's swell," says Frank as if it's settled. "You don't know how happy you've made me. You're coming for Christmas," he tells Henry Brown. "I'll show you the sights. I'll take you to school. Maybe I'll call you 'Brownie' for short."

"Maybe," says Ruthann. She means she wouldn't bet on it. But on which part wouldn't she bet?

"On the other hand," says Frank, "Henry Brown's a fine name. I'll just call him that."

That night Ruthann tells Henry Brown, "It's settled; your name is permanent. A pig your age doesn't need so much variety." Ruthann's parents overhear her and are pleased.

"Didn't we always say it was only a stage?" they say to each other.

Here come Frank's mother and father in their station wagon.

"It's big enough to hold a horse," says Frank's grandmother, as she watches them climb out.

"Thank you," says Frank's mother. She smiles as though she's heard a compliment. "How's our Frankie?"

"Fine," he says. "I'm fine."

His parents look around. The pig's the only livestock that they see. "Hi, Percival." Frank's mother recalls its name from last time. She is trying to be friendly. She gives a little wave in his direction.

"His name is Henry Brown," Frank tells her.

They all go inside. Ruthann's mother serves lemonade in the kitchen. "That's some pig," Frank's father says, watching it. Ruthann has poured part of her own lemonade into Henry Brown's dish. The dish is near the door. Henry Brown smacks his snout as he drinks. Frank, Jr., does not mention to his father his own plan about Henry Brown and Christmas. It is enough this minute to see his father warming up to the pig. Frank knows it's best to introduce any new idea slowly.

THERE GO Cousin Frank and Cousin Frank's parents in their station wagon, on their way home. Frank's small suitcase is in back. They have rolled up all the windows to keep out the dust. Dust makes Frank sneeze. Also, Frank's mother does not care to have the wind blow her hair.

"GOODBYE," THEY SAY, their voices muffled by the glass.

"Goodbye, goodbye," Ruthann and her parents and her grandmother say. Henry Brown grunts. He has seldom seen so much commotion.

"See you at Christmas," Frank calls. It is not precisely clear to whom he's calling. Could he be calling to the pig?

2

The Pig's Story

ALMOST AS SOON as Frank is gone, Ruthann begins to mull over his request. The idea does not appeal to her, but still she sees it's possible. Henry Brown didn't always live with her, after all. He used to live on the farm next door and belonged to Mr. Green. Visiting was how Ruthann got him in the first place. A pig that visited once *could* visit twice.

This was how that happened:

MR. GREEN was a pig farmer. He is retired now. He once raised pigs for a living and sold them to be eaten. Being eaten, however, turned out not to be Henry Brown's destiny. No doubt for that he is grateful. He certainly is obedient. The path his life took had a lot to do with his mother.

Henry Brown's mother was a thin, long-legged sort of a pig. She was a prize-winning pig, a blue-ribbon pig. She was Mr. Green's pride and joy. Mrs. Green, however, did not care much for her. She preferred a plumper sort of animal.

"She's a bit funny looking for a pig, don't you think?" she would ask her husband, gesturing widely with both hands in the air to indicate the portly sort of pig she favored. And not only that, but this particular pig, Henry Brown's mother, had the unfortunate habit of chasing after the pig farmer's wife whenever she came to feed it, which was twice every day. No wonder, then, Mrs. Green didn't care for it.

When Henry Brown was born the spitting image of his mother, Mrs. Green didn't care for him either. Certainly she didn't care to have two like that about the farm. She didn't even care to have the one, but Mr. Green was *that* attached to the elder pig that Mrs. Green knew there was no use complaining. He would never sell that one off the farm. The new piglet, though, was a different matter. It had not won any prize yet. Mr. Green was not attached to *it*.

"What would you think," the pig farmer's wife asked her husband one morning at breakfast, "of letting me have that new piglet out there in the pen for my own? The thin, long-legged one," she said. She could say this since the others in the farrow took after their father, athletic looking and less lean.

The pig farmer was surprised and pleased. He was surprised to see his wife take an interest in any pig at all. He was pleased she'd picked the best one in the litter. It was his favorite; a fine looking pig that took after its ma.

At first he said no, and what did she want it for anyway, and so on and so forth. He thought that if he drew a hard bargain, she'd value the pig that much more when it finally was hers. That's what he thought. He gave her the pig in the end.

Mrs. Green turned over in her mind what she could do with it. It was too young to sell for eating. Also, she knew her husband had his limits. He hadn't given it to her so that she could up and sell it off the farm the very first week that it was hers.

She waited several weeks. She weaned it from its mother with a baby bottle. She petted it to get it used to people. Then she bathed it, and brushed it, and tied a red plaid ribbon on its ear. It's the perfect pet, she said to herself, for that little girl next door, the one who

runs around with a squash all the time. She meant
Ruthann. Well, that was then.

"Come on, pig," Mrs. Green said, "we're going
visiting."

As you might imagine, Ruthann's squash had not escaped her parents' notice. A squash sitting at the dinner table every night is hard to overlook. "Summer of the squash," they would say in years to come, smiling, but they did not say that then.

"Why does she carry that squash everywhere?" they asked each other. Neither one knew. Of course they were asking the wrong person. They should have asked Ruthann. She would have told them. She had read about it in a book. Indian children in North Dakota did it. It struck her as a good idea. It still strikes her as a good idea, though now that she has a pig she doesn't need a squash too. But this was before Henry Brown.

Ruthann's squash was the sort that grows in two parts. It had a yellow head and a purple body. She picked it from her mother's garden. She had permission. Her mother never thought at the time to ask her what she planned to do with it.

Ruthann took that squash with her wherever she went. She carried it in her arms, undecorated and undressed. She sang songs and crooned lullabies and spoke to it as if it were a baby. Sometimes she tied a piece of colored cloth around herself and carried the squash wrapped in it on her back.

"Why does she do that?" Ruthann's aunt Lydia, wanted to know. "Maybe she'd like a doll," she suggested, as if no one before her had ever thought of it.

"She could open up a toy shop now," Ruthann's mam said, peeved. Naturally a doll had been the first thing she had tried.

"Perhaps the girl should see a doctor," suggested Ruthann's grandmother. She tapped one finger lightly to her forehead. She wanted no mistake about the sort of doctor that she meant.

"I'm sure it's just a stage," said Ruthann's mam. She tried to sound unworried. "Besides, it's bound to wilt." She meant that it would rot. No squash lasts forever.

It was, in any event, on account of that squash that Ruthann's mother found herself one summer day entertaining Mrs. Green who'd come visiting with her pig, and was offering to leave it. "It's a fine looking piglet," she said. "It would make a good pet for your daughter. Much better than that squash," she added, hoping to drive home her point.

Ruthann's mother regarded her guests a bit uncertainly. Mrs. Green sat comfortably on the living room sofa. The pig sat calmly at her feet. He was very mannerly. "I guess," Ruthann's mam said in a while, "that baby pig would be fine."

Ruthann was pleased to have him. The pig followed her wherever she went. She sang songs and crooned lullabies and spoke to him as if he understood her. She did try one time to wrap him in a blanket and carry him on her back, but he squirmed and scratched so hard she never tried it again. "You just walk along behind me then," she told him, and he did. It was a stroke of good luck for both of them that he had those long legs.

One day, quite by accident, the pig stepped on Ruthann's squash and squashed it. Ruthann didn't mind. It was already soft by then anyway, having been so long off the vine. "Never mind, pig," said Ruthann. "It's only a squash." Her parents overheard and were pleased.

"Didn't we always say it was only a stage?" they asked each other that night.

AND WHAT OF the pig farmer, Mr. Green? "It's a good-looking pig, isn't it?" he asks his wife whenever they walk by Ruthann and her pet on the road. Now that he's retired he has lots of time to walk. Mrs. Green always smiles and nods; her husband takes it for agreement.

3

Letters from Frank

IT IS SEVERAL weeks since Frank's visit. Ruthann, her mam, and Henry Brown are together in the kitchen. Outside, it is raining. "There's nothing like a rainy day for putting things in order," Ruthann's father said earlier that morning on his way to the attic.

"Right," said Ruthann's mam. She is pressing flowers. Stems and leaves are everywhere. Ruthann is practicing her painting. She is making a picture of her pig with watercolor paints she got for her birthday. A large puddle is forming on the table. Ruthann sees herself grown-up, an artist with an easel. She will hang a sign outside her door: "Ruthann Packer, Portraits a Specialty." Just as she is thinking this, the mailman comes and leaves a letter in their box. Ruthann goes to fetch it. It's from Cousin Frank, addressed to her parents.

August 13, 19__

Dear Aunt Hortense and Uncle Fritz,

How are you? I am fine. I am writing to thank you for having me as a guest on your farm. My mother says I should be grateful for the chance it gave me to breathe good, clean, country air, and I am. I had a wonderful time, especially after I stopped sneezing.

I hope I can visit again next summer. I will bring my swimming suit. Even though Ruthann said a person doesn't need one for a water hole, I will feel more comfortable in it. I know I have a lot to learn about swimming, including floating. I was glad that Ruthann did not push me in to teach me how, which she told me was one way to learn. I think it would not be the best way for me. My mother says she hopes that Ruthann does not swim in the same swimming hole with the pigs. "A person can get an earache," she says, "doing that." I explained to her that in the first place there is only one pig, and that in the second place the pig prefers the mud hole, so that is all right.

My mother says as long as I don't try diving she thinks the water will not bother my sinuses.

Please tell Ruthann I will write to her soon. I hope that she is thinking over my suggestion. If she does not remember my suggestion, please remind her for me that it had to do with Henry Brown and Christmas. That will jog her mind.

> Love,
> your nephew,
>
> Frank

A few days later another letter comes, this time addressed to Ruthann.

August 17, 19___

Dear Ruthann,

I wanted to write to you the same day that I wrote your parents so that I could mail both letters in one envelope, as I had only one stamp. What happened was that my letter to them turned out longer than I planned. By the time I finished it my hand had a cramp. Also, my mother wanted me to help fold laundry in our finished basement. You remember that we have a finished basement with a guest room no one uses. I checked it over carefully. I am positive Henry Brown would be comfortable in it. In the meantime, as you can see, I borrowed an extra stamp from my mother.

Have you decided yet about Henry Brown's visit? I know you have not had much time to think about it. Please keep in mind how much his visit would mean to me, and also that I am your only cousin in the world.

Love,
your cousin,

Frank

P.S.   Please send a snapshot for my wallet. If you have one of yourself with Henry Brown in it, please send that one. I look forward to a letter from you soon.

Letters begin arriving with some regularity. The mailman asks Ruthann if she has a beau. "No," she tells him. "It's just my cousin Frank."

September 3, 19___

Dear Ruthann,

I have not gotten any letter from you. Did you write one? My mother says sometimes a letter can get lost in the mail.

School starts next week in town. My father says probably it also starts next week in the country. What I worry about most is the school bus. Of course once school begins I may have worse problems I have not even thought of yet. But for now, the bus is the big one. My mother cannot see why it's a problem which means she either never had to go to school on a bus in her life, or she is so old she has forgotten what it was like. I have tried explaining to her.

"There are wild children on the bus," I have told her, "and bubble gum on the seats. Just wearing a hat is taking your life in your hands." Still she makes me wear one.

"If there is trouble," she says, "just tell the driver. That's what he's there for." Which goes to show how much she knows.

Once I took her advice, when I was younger. It was the day when the fourth and fifth graders were screeching at the tops of their lungs, "Kindergarten baby, kindergarten baby, stick your head in gravy," and at the same time, were trying to put our lunch-bags on over our heads. My lunch that day was sardines. I told the driver.

"Do I look like a policeman to you, sonny?" he asked. "I'm paid to drive the school bus. That's all I'm paid to do. Believe me, it isn't enough."

I realize a person such as yourself who has a pig like Henry Brown probably doesn't have problems on a school bus. Henry Brown probably walks you to your bus stop every morning, and meets you in the afternoon. Even Fatty Lipshitz would know better than to try and push around the owner of a pet like that. If I could sit next to Henry Brown on the school bus even once, I think my problems would be over. Please write back right away and let me know what you think.

Love,
your cousin,

September 21, 19___

Dear Ruthann,

Still no letter.

School has started. The bus is just as bad as I remembered. The big kids from last year are back, only bigger. Of course my mother made me wear my cap. I wore it in my pocket which did not help, as my pocket then stuck out and called attention to itself. My one hope now is that you will let Henry Brown visit. I am positive when Fatty and his friends see him sitting next to me on the bus they will ignore us, and even after Henry Brown has gone home, I will only need to remind them. "Watch your face," I'll say, "or I will bring my pig again tomorrow."

Our homework tonight is to write an essay, "What I Did During Summer Vacation." It is too bad you did not send a snapshot. I could have used it to illustrate my essay.

I will write again soon, and I hope you do the same.

Love,
your cousin,

Frank

P.S. If you find a snapshot of yourself and Henry Brown you can still send it. Even though it is too late for my essay, I could keep it in my wallet. If it is too big for my wallet, don't worry. I will tape it to the wall in our finished basement. That way Henry Brown will feel at home when he visits.

Love,
your cousin,

Frank

October 18, 19__

Dear Ruthann,

Thank you for your letter.

No, is the answer to your question. It is definitely not true that there are poisonous spiders in people's finished basements. Whoever told you that was lying, or else didn't know. Even my mother who is afraid to death of crawling animals watches television in the basement and does the laundry there. Believe me, if there was even the possibility of a poisonous spider, she would stay upstairs. If I were you, I would not even mention such a thing as a spider to her when you see her. Please remember me to Henry Brown.

Love,
your cousin,

Frank

October 27, 19__

Dear Ruthann,

We got back our essays on what we did last summer. I am sending you mine. I only got a *C* on it, which was not my fault. Even Ms. Grimes, my teacher, said she could tell it was sincere.

Sincerely yours,
your cousin,

Frank

WHAT I DID DURING SUMMER VACATION
AN ESSAY by Frank Packer

Last summer I spent a week at my cousin Ruthann's farm. Ruthann has a pet pig. You might not think a pig would be such a good pet, but that is only because you have not met Henry Brown which you probably will this Christmas, if he comes to my house to visit. I will bring him with me to school one time on the school bus so everyone can meet him. He is a very well-trained pig and certainly he is housebroken. He does not bark or have fleas like a dog. He has no bad habits that I know about. I am positive that if he had any, they would have shown up during the week I spent with him on the farm, but nothing did.

A pig would be a good pet for anyone with enough room to keep it. We have enough room at our house if you count the backyard and the finished basement, which is where Henry Brown will sleep when he comes. Also, a pig is the best pet in the world for a person with allergies like me. I have never heard of a single person who ever was allergic to a pig. Of course I am speaking about a pet pig only, not the kind you eat which Henry Brown will never ever be.

The End

P.S.   Ms. Grimes said that if the essay was supposed to have been about pets, mine would have been very good. "Next time, Franklin," she said, "stay on the topic." Also, she said, it was hard for her to read my handwriting. Personally, I do not think it is fair for my grade to depend on handwriting. That is what penmanship is for and I am already almost failing it. I hope you let me know soon about Henry Brown. Keep in mind that I have practically promised my teacher he will be here. It will not help my progress in school if he doesn't show up. As you can see, I need all the help that I can get.

P.P.S.   My mother made my father ride the school bus last week. "I cannot believe," she said, "that it can be as bad as Frank describes it." "It wasn't so bad," my father said. Well of course not. My father is almost six feet tall and overweight. No one took his hat or tried to trip him. "Have a good day," the driver told him when he got off the bus.

November 20, 19___

Dear Ruthann,
     Thank you for the Thanksgiving Day card. The turkey picture that you drew is very nice. I do not

agree, however, that a turkey would make a better pet in town than a pig. Are you forgetting about my allergy to feathers? Or that I have already told everyone in school about Henry Brown? How would it look to have a turkey instead of a pig sitting next to me on the school bus? I think that probably I would never live it down.

I was glad to hear about Petunia's kittens. My mother says she's not surprised; that that's the way it is with cats. She once took in a stray. "That cat is going to have kittens," all the neighbors said. My

mother took it to the veterinarian. "Oh, no," he told
her. "That cat is not going to have kittens. She is almost a kitten herself." My mother kept her. A few
weeks later she had four kittens underneath the cov-
ers, in my mother's bed. My mother found homes for
all five of them. "But it wasn't easy," she said. Maybe
I could give Ms. Grimes one of Petunia's kittens as a
surprise for Christmas. It could travel here with
Henry Brown. Please write soon and let me know
what you think. As my mother says, "The holidays
are almost upon us and what do you want to give
Ruthann for Christmas?"

Love,
your cousin,

Frank

December 8, 19___

Dear Ruthann,
My mother says that we will be spending Christmas with you on the farm. It is a good thing she told
me, because if I had to count on you for such news I
would still be in the dark. I have not heard a word
from you yet about Henry Brown, but I am sure you

can see how convenient it would be with the new plans. He could come home with us after Christmas in the station wagon.

My mother says I cannot surprise my teacher with a kitten for Christmas. I have not found anyone so far to take one. The children I know whose parents like cats already have some. "One more would be too many," their parents tell them, "even if it is only a little kitten."

As time is getting short, and you have not written since before Thanksgiving, I will just hope for the best. I am fixing up the guest room in the finished basement for Henry Brown. I will choose your Christmas present by myself and bring it in the station wagon when we come.

Love,
your cousin,

Frank

P.S.   I have not mentioned a word about our plans yet to my parents. My mother would only worry for no reason. "A pig in town, Frank?" she'd probably ask. "How do you know he won't get carsick? Can Henry Brown even climb down and up stairs? Will he be allowed to ride on the school bus? Perhaps you haven't thought this through enough." Having thought it all through carefully, I think that the best thing is not to say a word until we're leaving. Then we can quietly lead Henry Brown to the station wagon and put him inside. If they notice him there and ask, then we'll explain. Have you talked about our plans yet with Henry Brown?

P.P.S. Probably we will have to write an essay after Christmas on "What I Did During My Christmas Vacation." Having Henry Brown come home with me, I think, will help my grade a lot.

Love,
your cousin,

Frank

4

Grandmother Packer and Her Boys

DOES HENRY BROWN or doesn't Henry Brown go to town after Christmas? That is the question. And if he goes, how does he like it in the finished basement? Well, *perhaps* that is the question. On the other hand, the real question may be, if Henry Brown stays home, does someone else go in his place? First, to answer that, we need to find out more about this family. Where did Ruthann's and Frank's grandmother come from to begin with? And what about their grandfather; where has he been all these years?

"That's what I'd like to know," says the children's grandmother. That is what this next part is about.

Here come Ruthann and her pig.

Ruthann has a package tucked under one arm. It is a large, flat package wrapped in brown paper and tied up with string. She has just bought Henry Brown his Christmas present.

Ruthann's grandmother is visiting again. She has brought her hurdy-gurdy and is in the living room playing it. Her hurdy-gurdy is from the old country. Ruthann's grandmother is also from the old country. She carried her hurdy-gurdy on the boat coming here. Her two boys came with her.

Ruthann puts her package on the table and sits down to listen to her grandmother make music. Henry Brown sits down and listens too. Petunia and her kittens have been listening all along.

Ruthann's grandmother likes to make music. Well, she likes it *now*. When she did it in the old days for a living, she didn't like it that much *then*. "That was some breeze on those corners," she says, meaning the street corners in Romania where she played. She was a street musician. "When it wasn't so cold that your fingers froze, it was summertime and much too hot. It was hard just to keep the hurdy-gurdy in tune. So many pigeons came by. It was a good thing that I had my parrot," she once told Ruthann. " 'Parrot wants a cracker!' it would shout, and scare away the pigeons. They were not used to talking birds. Also, it was good for business. People stopped to see the parrot and stayed to hear the music. They sometimes bought a painting."

"Don't you mean, 'Polly wants a cracker'?" Ruthann asked. We will come back to the painting in a minute.

"I beg your pardon," said her grandmother.

"I said," Ruthann repeated, "probably your parrot said, 'Polly wants a cracker.' " She put it this new way so that it would not sound like contradicting.

"Are you contradicting?" asked her grandmother, a bit put out. "The bird's name was Parrot. Why would it say Polly? 'Parrot wants a cracker' was what he said when he was hungry. . . ."

"WHAT'S THAT in your package?" her grandmother asks in a while.

"What package?" Ruthann has nearly forgotten it. "Oh, *that* package," she says, seeing where her grandmother is pointing with the cane she uses in cold or rainy weather. On warm, sunny days her legs work fine.

Ruthann removes the package from the table and unties the string. She pulls the paper off and holds up a picture so that her grandmother can see it.

The picture is unframed.

"Oh, my," her grandmother says, staring. "It looks so familiar." To say that she seems surprised would be an understatement.

"Of course it looks familiar," says Ruthann. "It's Henry Brown. I had him drawn in charcoal. It's his Christmas present. I plan to hang it up beside the watercolor of him that I painted."

"Sure, Henry Brown," says her grandmother. "But what I mean is that the *style* looks so familiar. Where did you get it?"

"School Street and Lime," says Ruthann proudly. "It was drawn to order."

"It reminds me of your grandfather," says her grandmother.

"Henry Brown reminds you of my grandfather?" Ruthann is astonished.

"Don't be silly," says her grandmother. "The *technique* reminds me of your grandfather. He was some artist. He made portraits for a living. I played and he painted. We worked the same street corners. He painted portraits of my customers. Sometimes they'd buy one. When there were no customers he drew portraits of my parrot. Sometimes he drew pigeons. After he finished a drawing, he always signed it with his initials. He hid them in the picture.

"Just like this," says Ruthann's grandmother, pointing. She is pointing at Henry Brown's ear in the portrait. She puts on her eyeglasses. She traces with one finger the two initials she sees there: *F. P.* They are the initials of Ruthann's father. They are *his* father's initials. Can it mean something? Or is it only a coincidence?

"The artist," she asks Ruthann, "who drew this portrait, exactly what did he look like?" Perhaps she really means, *Who did he look like?* Did he look like a member of their family for instance? Could he be her long lost husband?

"He was old," says Ruthann. "He had gray hair and a beard. His eyes were very blue, and he wore glasses."

"Was he short?"

Ruthann can't be certain. "He was sitting on a wooden crate. I think if he had stood, he would have been as tall as you." Ruthann's grandmother is a very short person.

She nods. It's good enough for her. She is not *that* surprised. "I always felt," she says, more to herself than Ruthann, "he'd show up one day."

Thoughtfully, she plays her hurdy-gurdy. "Better late than never" is not a saying that she holds with. The question is, who needs him now? Once, she did. They all did once, but that was long ago. They needed him that day, for instance, when they arrived by boat, she and her two boys, and landed in New York. He'd come on ahead. He was to have met them at the pier. They looked for him. He wasn't there. They waited in Manhattan and brushed up on their English. Months went by. Then Ruthann's grandmother shrugged. "I guess we're on our own," she told her boys. She'd had time by then to see the city and decide. It was not the sort of place she cared to raise her sons.

"How would you like to be peasants?" she asked Frank and Fritz. She meant farmers, of course. "Peasants" was what they were called in Romania. Well, what did they know, boys of seven and nine? Besides, they thought she'd said pheasants. They talked it over. It sounded good to them, flying about the countryside in pretty, colored feathers. They said "sure." The next thing they knew they were riding a train to the country.

"Are we in the country yet?" their mother asked the conductor every few stops.

"When you see pigs and chickens," he said, "you'll know that you're there." That was why they got off the train the very first pig they saw.

Life wasn't easy in the country for a woman on her own with two sons. She was glad she'd left the parrot behind with her sister. It was one less mouth to feed. She put aside her hurdy-gurdy and hired herself out to a farmer. She went to night school to improve her gram-

mar. When her boys were not in school, they had their chores and odd jobs which brought in extra money. "Though goodness knows, we still were poor," all of them will say, remembering. "Well, there was always enough to eat, and the boys had their pets," their mother recalls. "It was a good sight better than the city." It was also a bit of good luck for her that Frank and Fritz were short. They hardly ever outgrew clothing. By the time they shot up in high school, they both had regular jobs and paid their own expenses.

The first year she advertised: "Fritz and Frank Packer and their mother have arrived from Romania. They can be contacted at _____ ." Here she put the RFD number and the name of the farm where they were staying. She hoped her husband, or someone who knew his whereabouts, would see the ad and contact them.

No one did. Through the years she wondered what had happened to her husband. She wondered less as time went by.

The boys missed their father. They vowed when they grew up they'd go find him. But the years passed, and a day finally came when they saw themselves complete, a family of three. Even so, Fritz sometimes said to Frank, "It would be nice to have someone around to call 'Pop.'" "It would be nice," Frank sometimes said to Fritz, "to have a father to kick around a football with, or shoot baskets." Every June they had to make Father's Day cards in school. "You must know some nice man with no children to give it to," their teachers told them. Every year the cards got misplaced somehow or other on the way home from school.

"GRANDFATHER'S BACK," Ruthann announces to her father toward evening, the minute he sets foot in the door.

"What's that you say, Ruthie?" he asks. He closes the door behind Rover.

Ruthann's mother explains what they know. It isn't that much, but it's something. She holds up Henry Brown's portrait. She points to the initials. "It's just an outside chance," she says. "A very long shot."

Ruthann's father examines the portrait. He nods in

a serious way. He looks as though he's carefully considering the facts. He lays the portrait on the table with due deliberation. He sees himself as a mature and sober person, a man who does not rush headlong to a conclusion. He walks slowly to the telephone. He raises its receiver. He dials his brother's number.

"POP IS BACK! POP IS BACK! DO YOU HEAR ME, FRANK? POP IS BACK!" He is shouting like a maniac. At the same time he is holding his left ankle in his left hand at hip level and hopping up and down in place on his right foot. Ruthann has never seen him look so undignified. Her grandmother has. He hopped this same way years ago, on stage, in a school play. He was supposed to be a rose in bloom then. "Of course you can do it," his teacher told him. "Just don't move a muscle."

"Pop who?" asks his brother.

"Our pop. Pop Packer. He's standing on the corner." He means the corner of School Street and Lime, where Ruthann first saw him. "He drew Ruthie a picture of her pig. I'd know him anywhere." Well, sure, he'd know the pig. He sees it every day. But what about the man? He tells his brother the few details he knows. "We're on our way to find him now. We'll call when we get back." Tears of joy overflow his eyes. "Do you know how many times I've dreamed that this would happen, that our father would come home!"

Ruthann's mother looks worried. She is worried that her husband is heading for a heartbreak. She does not believe in jumping to conclusions. She is both right and wrong. She is right in principle, but wrong in this case. Sometimes jumping works, and sometimes it doesn't. Ruthann's father tucks Henry Brown's portrait under one arm and rushes from the house.

"I'll just wait here until you get back," Ruthann's grandmother calls behind him. She wants to practice playing her hurdy-gurdy. "I've gotten rusty in America," she tells the cat. In case the artist really is her husband, she doesn't want to disappoint him. For all she knows, he has a perfectly good explanation for why he never met them. Perhaps he didn't get her cable. Or couldn't read her ads. Whoever said he went to night school to learn English?

Here come Ruthann's mother and father, Ruthann, Henry Brown, and Rover.

They are riding in their pickup truck. They arrive at the corner of School Street and Lime. A small crowd is gathered. They join it. It encircles an old man with gray hair, a beard, and very blue eyes. He has on glasses. He

is putting final touches on a portrait of a little girl and her toy turtle. Now he is finished. He wraps the drawing in brown paper, ties it with string, and gives it to the girl. He packs up his charcoals and pencils. He folds his easel. The crowd departs. Except Ruthann and her parents, Henry Brown, and Rover remain. Ruthann's father holds up Henry Brown's portrait.

"Hey," he says. "This is the best looking portrait I've ever seen."

The artist looks at it, and then at Henry Brown. "Hey," he says, with a heavy accent. "That is the best looking pig I've ever seen." Ruthann could not agree more.

"Thank you," she tells him.

Ruthann's father intends to say next, "Why don't you come home with us and have dinner?" He has some questions he would like to ask this man. Instead he cries: "POP! POP! MY DEAREST POP! ALL MY LIFE I'VE LOOKED FOR YOU!" He throws himself into the artist's arms. The old man still is sitting. Ruthann's father is sitting on his lap. The artist looks confused.

"Just wait," says Ruthann's father, "until Frankie hears about this." He means his brother Frank.

Ruthann's mam explains to the artist what she knows. She is still not certain that Ruthann's father has found the right father, although it is true there is a resemblance. They both have the same blue eyes and the same cleft chin. So has Ruthann.

"If I saw him on the street," Ruthann's mam says, "he'd certainly look familiar."

"You are seeing him on the street," Ruthann points out.

The artist, who in fact is Ruthann's grandfather, appears to think over what he has been told. Then he says, "Well, isn't that nice." Nice, thinks Ruthann. Is that all he can say? In this way, she sees he is not entirely like his son. Also, when he stands, he hardly comes above Ruthann's father's shoulder.

After dinner that evening, Ruthann's grandfather tells about his life in America. You would think, her grandmother thinks, he might want to know about mine, mine and the boys'. "Every town I painted in," he says, "I looked for you. Every bus I rode," he says, "I thought of you. Not a day went by," he says, "that I did not yearn for you."

Ruthann's father beams. He believes every word.

Ruthann's grandmother would like to believe her husband's story. He is family after all, and her boys' father. Life in America has made her cautious, though, and she reserves judgment.

Ruthann's mam knows there are telephone books in libraries. The Packers all have listed numbers. None of them, she thinks, would have been that hard to find. She keeps her mouth closed so her thoughts won't escape her.

Ruthann believes. She believes in romance. This is the most romantic thing that has ever happened in her life. "Wait until Frank hears about this," she tells Henry Brown. She means her cousin Frank. She hopes it will wipe all thoughts of Henry Brown's Christmas visit from his mind. She is not counting on it, though.

"So," she asks her grandfather, "what should I call you?"

"Call me Grandda," he says. "That's who I am."

5

Christmas Comes Early

RUTHANN'S FAMILY has decided to celebrate Christmas early this year. "It isn't every day of the week a boy finds his dad," Ruthann's father said on the telephone to his brother Frank. He says it several times a day now. He says it to Ruthann's grandmother and grandfather, to Ruthann's mam, to Ruthann, and now and then to Rover. Except for Rover, who barks back, the rest of them have given up replying. Ruthann's mam and grandparents are busy making preparations for the holiday, and Ruthann is busy making up her mind. She tries hard to be fair and always look at both sides of every question. She is making a list:

HENRY BROWN GOES TO TOWN

Reasons for

1. It would make Frank happy.

2. It would be only for a week or two.

3. Henry Brown might like a change of scene.

4. Frank would take good care of him.

5. There are no spiders in Frank's basement.

Reasons against

1. I'd miss Henry Brown.

2. Henry Brown would miss me. He might think I'd given him away forever.

3. What if he forgets me?

4. Frank might forget fresh water. Or overfeed him. He isn't used to pigs.

5. There are no windows. It must be dark down there, and damp. Henry Brown could catch pneumonia.

Ruthann pauses to reflect. Henry Brown might hate it there. What if he escaped, and ran away, tried to get back home? He could get lost. Or have an accident. He could get run over crossing a street. Or eaten. Or run over and eaten. Ruthann is horrified.

"That's that," she says to Henry Brown. "You're staying home. It's much too dangerous in town for a pig." Ruthann's only problem now is how to tell Frank without hurting his feelings.

She seeks advice from her mam. Her mam is understanding. "I understand," she tells Ruthann. She is also no help whatsoever. "Just say no," she says. She still believes that short and to the point is best.

Ruthann confides in her grandmother. Her grandmother does not understand Ruthann's decision. "I think you ought to think again," she advises. "A trip to town would do that pig a world of good. It would teach him to appreciate the farm." Well, Henry Brown already appreciates the farm. Ruthann's grandmother is really only thinking it would be heaven not to trip over a pig for a change.

Ruthann turns to her father for guidance. He is glad to help. Isn't that what a father is for? "Ask your grandda," he advises. "He's a man with ideas."

Ruthann explains the situation to her grandfather. She shows him Frank's letters. "Henry Brown can't go

to town," she says. "I'd miss him much too much."
Ruthann's grandfather thinks it over, and comes up
with a plan. He tells it to her.

"What a good idea!" she says. "But will it work?"

"We won't know until we try it."

Ruthann explains the plan to Henry Brown. "We'll
just have to cross our fingers and hope for the best,"
she tells him.

Here come Frank and his parents now, pulling up in their station wagon.

Frank is wheezing slightly for no apparent reason. "I think it's the cold air," his mother says, fixing her hair. Her hair is a new color, and Ruthann has to look twice to be positive it is her same aunt Lydia.

The Christmas tree is already up and decorated. By the next morning presents are under it for everyone. A sweater is there for Henry Brown. Ruthann's mother knit it. Frank is allergic to pine needles, so he must sit as far from the tree as he can, in a corner of the room.

"I'm sorry I didn't get you a present." He apologizes to Ruthann. "I only found out the night before last we were having Christmas early this year." Frank looks gloomy because of his allergy. He brightens only now and then when he looks at Henry Brown.

"Don't worry," Ruthann tells him. She is feeling sorrier for him by the minute. A pig seems such a small request. If only it weren't *her* pig. She regards Henry Brown in his new red sweater. How handsome he looks. How happy Ruthann is that he is staying home.

"So, Frankie," says Grandda. "I understand you'd like a pig to visit." Well, Frank is right this minute visiting a pig. His grandfather means, of course, that

Frank would like a visit from a pig, from Henry Brown. "It's not so healthy for a pig in town. You'd need to look out for the neighbors every minute. All the time they'd be complaining. Ruthann and I have something else for you," Grandda says. "Better than a pig. Also, more portable."

It is hard for Frank to imagine anything better than a pig. Still, he looks interested. Ruthann and Grandda go inside. They come back carrying a large square of canvas between them. They turn it around so Frank can see it. Is he ever surprised! It is a large oil painting of Henry Brown. Ruthann and Frank are standing on either side of him. Grandda stayed up late last night to finish Frank. He'd had only a photograph to go by until then. Henry Brown is wearing tusks. He looks rather fierce for such a nice pig. Grandda's initials are hidden in the painting. So are Ruthann's.

"It's wonderful," says everyone in the room, all together.

"There is certainly no shortage of pig portraits in this house," says Aunt Lydia. She means, of course, beside this new one, the charcoal and the watercolor.

"Why does Henry Brown have on tusks?" asks Frank.

"Ah," says his grandfather. "I thought you'd notice. Ruthann put them there. Tusks were her idea. All attack pigs have them. The painting is your Christmas present.

You'll take it to school on the bus. When that fat boy bully sees it, then you'll tell him: 'This is an attack pig. It's my Christmas present. He's still on the farm getting trained. After he is, he's coming to town.' "

"But will he believe me?" Frank asks.

"He'll have to," says his grandda. "I'll be right there next to you to make sure. So will your grandmother," he adds, seeing how she's looking at him. "We're going back with you to visit."

Frank is glad to hear it. Even so, he'd feel more confident if his grandda were a little taller.

6

Grandda Rides the School Bus

Here come Frank and his grandfather and his grandmother.

They are getting on the school bus. Someone is giving them a hand. Frank is carrying his painting Grandda holds his folded easel. The hurdy-gurdy must be tipped to get it through the door.

"Do you have a school bus pass?" the driver wants to know. Frank's grandparents do not.

"I'll overlook it just this one time," the driver tells them.

64

"Hey, what's this?" Fatty has grabbed Frank's portrait and is holding it up.

"It's Frankie's Christmas present," says Grandda.

"Frankie?" Fatty lifts an eyebrow. Frank's heart sinks. He can hear that name repeated in that same soprano tone for the rest of his life, at least until high school. "Hey, Frankie," Fatty says, "that's some pig."

"It's an attack pig," Frank's grandfather explains. "You can tell by its tusks. It's still on the farm getting trained. After that, who knows? A visit to town may just be his ticket." Frank's grandfather is standing in the aisle looking for some place to set his easel. He finds one, then sits beside Frank's grandmother who is cradling her hurdy-gurdy in her lap. He looks Fatty up and down. "I bet a boy like you," he says, "could use a pig like that. We both could use a pig like Frank's." Before Fatty can ask why, Grandda tells him. "Short people like us," he says, "want some protection."

Fatty is taken by surprise. "Who does he mean is short?" He seems to be asking any rider on the bus.

"Some tall people," Grandda says, as if in answer to a question, "like to pick on short people. No one knows why. It's an unsolved mystery."

Fatty, puzzled, still is standing, looking all around. "I'm not short. Who is he calling short?" he asks his best friend, "Bug."

Bug shrugs. Grandda goes on talking. "I myself am a short person. You," he says to Fatty, "are a smidgen shorter. I saw it right away when we were standing. If you want me to, I'll stand again and we can measure."

"Sit down in the back of the bus!" the driver yells. Fatty sits down across the aisle from Grandda. They carry on their conversation.

"I'm only twelve," Fatty explains. "I'm tall for twelve."

"Sure, you're tall now," Grandda says. "I was once tall, too. When I was twelve, I was tall for my age. 'What a nice tall boy,' people used to tell my mother. That was the same year I stopped growing."

Frank's grandmother leans over to pat Fatty's hand. "Don't worry, sonny," she tells him. "If it isn't in your nature to be short, you won't be. Both my boys were short until high school. You should see them now." Well, Fatty has already seen Frank's father. He puffs out his chest and puts on a brave face. Frank thinks he looks a little worried.

When the bus stops in front of the school, everyone gets off except the driver. "Make sure you have a pass next time," he tells Frank's grandparents as they haul the easel and the hurdy-gurdy down the steps. He does not say, "Have a nice day."

Frank introduces his grandparents to Ms. Grimes, his teacher, and to his classmates, and to Ms. Hanes, the principal. His grandmother plays the hurdy-gurdy for his class and tells about Romania. His grandfather draws pencil sketches of the children. Frank holds up his portrait of himself, Ruthann, and Henry Brown.

"Come back again," Ms. Grimes says when school is over. She writes out a school bus pass for Frank's grandparents. "Use it any time," she tells them. She thinks that they are the most colorful people she has ever met. She can hardly wait to rush home and tell her husband all about them.

"So, your parents named you Fatty," Grandda says on the school bus going home. "It's an interesting name."

"No one names a baby Fatty. It's my nickname," Fatty answers.

"You don't say!" says Grandda. He looks surprised. "I sometimes have a nickname myself," he says. " 'Shorty.' Sometimes in English, sometimes in Romanian. My real name is Packer. Mr. Felix Packer. What's your real name?"

"Roland," says Fatty. "Roland Christian Lipshitz." Frank is amazed. He didn't know that. Why has Fatty's real name been a secret until now?

"If we were friends," Grandda tells him, "I could call you R.C."

Fatty stares at him. "R.C.," he says in a while. "I like it."

"Sure you do," says Grandda. "It has a nice ring."

Slowly, R.C. starts to smile.

"He's a good-looking boy when he smiles," Frank's grandmother says to anyone.

"You seem like a nice boy," Grandda tells Fatty. "I like you. You can call me Grandda."

"You're not his grandda," Frank says when they are off the bus.

"Of course not. But, Frankie, if he calls me that I think he won't put sardines on your head so soon again." Put that way, Frank sees it makes sense.

Here comes Frank.

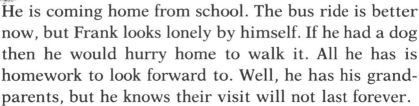

He is coming home from school. The bus ride is better now, but Frank looks lonely by himself. If he had a dog then he would hurry home to walk it. All he has is homework to look forward to. Well, he has his grandparents, but he knows their visit will not last forever.

"Your homework is to write an essay," Ms. Grimes

told the class. "The topic is, 'What I Did During Christmas Vacation.' " The class was not surprised.

"You look a little gloomy, Frank," his grandfather says when Frank gets home. "A boy like you should have a dog." He means an only child should have a pet. He says it as if no one before him ever thought of it, as if he's never heard of such a thing as an allergy.

Frank is too glum to reply.

"Maybe a Mexican hairless," his grandda goes on. "It's bred in Mexico. It has no hair."

Frank looks interested. He is interested in even just knowing how ·his grandfather knows of such a dog.

"There's more to life than night school," his grandfather tells him. "I haven't just been sitting on my thumbs. I've painted all across America, including Mexico. I've painted dogs. 'Any time you want a pup, just ask,' a breeder told me. He was *that* pleased with my portrait of his. Naturally, I couldn't take one then. A puppy, even with no hair, can get a man put off a bus. 'Write when you get ready,' Señor Perez said. Now might be the time. First, we have to ask your mother."

Frank's mother is in the den balancing her checkbook. She looks up as they come in. "A Mexican hairless would be just the right dog in a family like this," Frank's

grandfather tells her.
"Nothing to shed; no reason
to sneeze."

"Ummm," she says. She promises to think about it.
"It would certainly be better than a pig," she tells
Frank's father when he gets home from work.

That night, Frank's grandfather writes to his friend
in Mexico. Frank writes his essay on "What I Did During
Christmas Vacation." He illustrates it.

WHAT I DID DURING CHRISTMAS VACATION

by Frank Packer

Our family celebrated Christmas early this year on the farm, which you already know about from my essay, "What I Did During Summer Vacation."

We celebrated early because of my grandfather's showing up. He had been missing for years and years, since my grandmother came to this country and couldn't find him. After the first year, she gave up looking. Now at last my father has someone to send a Father's Day card.

I am sorry to report that Ruthann's pig, Henry Brown, did not come home with me. My grandmother and grandfather came instead. He is an artist and she plays the hurdy-gurdy, as you know from having met them. She is also a farmer. I guess now he will be a farmer too. They are a family of farmers, except for my father. He works in an office. He has a computer on his desk. It prints out important information on long white rolls of paper. What he does with all this information, I have no idea.

Meantime, there is good news. My grandfather has not been sitting on his thumbs all these years. He has painted all across America. He is writing to his friend in Mexico, Señor Perez, who raises hairless dogs. His friend may send me one. If he does, I will bring him to school to meet you.

This is what I did during Christmas vacation.

The End

Frank's essay is returned with a *C*.

"A *C*. Again, a *C*," his mother says. Frank himself finds it hard to believe. "You must learn to keep to the topic," is written in red at the top; also, "You seem to have a flair for art." Ms. Grimes is referring to Frank's illustrations. She makes no mention of his penmanship, for which he is grateful.

The same week that Frank gets back his essay, his grandparents leave for their farm. The day before they do, his grandfather waits for Frank at the bus stop, after school, so he can say goodbye to R.C. "I'm counting on you to look out for Frank," Grandda tells him. What he's really counting on, however, is an early spring. Then R.C. will have other things on his mind, baseball for instance. When fall comes, he'll be in Junior High and ride a different bus to school. R.C. and Grandda shake hands. Already, R.C. seems a smidgen taller.

THAT NIGHT Frank writes Ruthann a letter to bring her up to date. He encloses his illustrated essay. Ruthann writes back to thank him.

7

Letters from Ruthann

February 2, 19__

Dear Frank,

Happy Groundhog Day. It is raining on the farm. If any groundhog does come out, there won't be any shadow.

Thank you for your letter, and the essay. The illustrations are a good late Christmas present. I hung them next to the two portraits of Henry Brown already in the kitchen. My mother said your teacher is certainly right about one thing. "That boy has a flair for art," she said. "He must get it from his grandda." I reminded her about my watercolors. She said, "I guess Ruthann has her grandda's eye for color."

Grandmother was visiting. "They certainly didn't get my ear for music," she said. "Beside the two of them, that pig has talent." I think she is still holding against us that time you got the end of my braid caught in her hurdy-gurdy.

Have you heard about your dog yet? I found this out in the library: Hairless dogs have been bred in Mexico for thousands of years, or else they came with sailors from China centuries ago. No one knows. Once they were raised in flocks, like turkeys, then eaten. Now they are raised purely for pets, like Henry Brown. They are supposed to be rubbed down every night with baby oil, then covered with blankets while they sleep. This would seem to leave out staying in a finished basement.

Love,

Ruthann

P.S. March 1st is National Pig Day. I found that out in the library too. I am planning to bake a cake for Henry Brown.

March 8, ____

Dear Frank,

Thank you for your National Pig Day card. My mother said she wasn't surprised you couldn't find one in the store. Personally, I think a homemade card is much better. Grandda helped me bake the cake. I helped Henry Brown blow out the candles. I hope you like the snapshot.

78

I was happy to hear about your dog flying up next month from Mexico. Be sure to send a picture. I think having him sleep in bed with you is an excellent idea.

No, is the answer to your question. I do not mind if you name him H.B. I am sure Henry Brown will be proud to have such a namesake.

Love,

Ruthann

P.S. Have you mentioned the sleeping arrangements to your mother yet?

April 10, ____

Dear Frank,

How did H.B. enjoy his plane ride?

I have not gotten any mail from you lately. I do realize training an animal takes up quite a bit of time. Even so, I hope that you will send a letter soon, and enclose a picture of H.B.

Love,

Ruthann

May 1, 19__

Dear Frank,

    Thank you for your letter and the picture.

    Henry Brown and I are looking forward to your visit this summer, and also to meeting H.B. Don't forget your swimming suit. Maybe you should pack it now so that it won't get left out at the last minute.

Love,

Ruthann

P.S. I was glad to hear that R.C. will be on a different bus next year. I know he seems reformed, but a person can fall behind over the summer.

8
The Swimming Hole

Here come Ruthann and Henry Brown and Frank and his dog, H.B.

Ruthann's father is bringing up the rear. Even though it is summertime, H.B. is wearing a lightweight sweater. Ruthann and Frank are in their swimming suits. Henry Brown is as he always is. Frank is getting used to seeing him this way again, tuskless. Ruthann's father is dressed in blue jeans, a plaid shirt, and a straw hat. He has come along to supervise the swimming lesson.

"Don't let Frank get water in his nose," Ruthann's

mother called behind them as they left. She had in mind his sinuses.

Frank has in mind his essay, "What I Did During Summer Vacation." He wrote it before leaving for the farm. He hoped in that way to be able to stick to the topic. So far, all of it is true. He plans to illustrate it with a picture of the swimming hole, himself leaping into it. Ruthann has offered to let him use her watercolors.

Ruthann looks very happy. She begins to skip.

Ruthann's father smiles, watching all of them. Then he starts to sing: "Old Fritz Packer has a farm, E-I-E-I-O." Henry Brown pricks up his ears, and then slows down. He looks so peaceful strolling in the meadow, listening to the song.